W9-CIO-109

The WORRYSAURUS

For little River & Baby Sky . . .
may you always find a way to set
your butterflies free x
R.B.

For Akshay & Rian

C.C.

Text copyright © 2019 by Rachel Bright
Illustrations copyright © 2019 by Chris Chatterton

All rights reserved. Published by Scholastic Inc., *Publishers since 1920.*
SCHOLASTIC and associated logos are trademarks and/or registered trademarks of Scholastic Inc.

The publisher does not have any control over and does not assume any
responsibility for author or third-party websites or their content.

No part of this publication may be reproduced, stored in a retrieval system,
or transmitted in any form or by any means, electronic, mechanical, photocopying,
recording, or otherwise, without written permission of the publisher.
For information regarding permission, write to Scholastic Inc., Attention:
Permissions Department, 557 Broadway, New York, NY 10012.

ISBN 978-1-338-72959-7

10 9 8 7 6 5 4 3   20 21 22 23 24

Printed in the U.S.A.   141
First edition, September 2020

RACHEL BRIGHT

CHRIS CHATTERTON

The
WORRYSAURUS

Scholastic Inc.

On a hot and sunny morning,
under lovely clear blue skies,
A little Worrysaurus was
opening his eyes.

He brushed his tiny
POINTY TEETH,

then washed his
TOP AND TAIL.

He packed a little
BAG OF SNACKS
and set off on a trail.

He skipped along with happy legs,
across the golden sand,
And thought about the day that
he had plotted, sketched, and planned.

A lovely
YUMMY picnic, a
DELICIOUS
summer spread.

DINO BITES

Worrysaurus liked
it when he knew
what lay ahead.

But he hadn't gotten far, you see,
it hadn't been that long,
Before his busy head dreamed up
some things that might go wrong . . .

Had he made enough to **EAT** today?

And brought enough to **DRINK?**

This Worrysaurus often was a one to **OVERTHINK.**

"What if I get **LOST?**" he thought,
"Or trip and have a fall?"

His happy legs were slowing to a
SNUFFLY, SHUFFLY CRAWL.

Worrysaurus liked it when he felt he
was prepared. Unexpected happenings . . .
they made him feel quite

SCARED.

So when . . .

... suddenly from nowhere, a lizard **SKITTERED** by,

shouting in a squeaky **YELP**

and pointing at the sky:

"I think a STORM is coming!
I heard it's on its way!"

Well, that REALLY put a cloud
above his Worrysaurus day.

"A storm?" said Worrysaurus,
"When it's so dry and hot and sunny?"
BUT the news became a butterfly
that flittered in his tummy.

"I'm NOT READY
for the rain," he said.

"I haven't got my wellies!"

His teeth began to **CHATTER** and his knees — they turned to JELLIES.

And all the while, the sky was blue!
The sun it shone and shone.
But now his lovely picnic thoughts
were definitely gone.

Should he

find a cave

to shelter?

Or

RUN back home

and HIDE?

His little worry butterfly
grew very strong inside.

But then he thought of something
that his mommy liked to say:

"Oh, my
little Worrysaurus,

CHASE THAT BUTTERFLY AWAY!

Don't you worry now, my lovely,
you **MUST** try not to fret.
If it's not a happy ending,
then it hasn't ended yet."

So he reached into his bag just then, to find a little tin.

It helped him with his worries — it had **HAPPY THINGS** within.

A **SPECIAL STICK,**

his **TEDDY NED,**

a **PEBBLE,**

My lovely little brave one
I'm so very proud of

and a **LETTER.**

And he held them
ONE BY ONE...

so everything felt better.

Then he put away his tin
and all the worries
in his head . . .
FREED his little
butterfly for happy
thoughts instead.

"I'll stand
up **TALL**.
I can be
STRONG.

I'LL CHASE MY FEARS AWAY!

All is good and all is well

and everything's OK."

And with those
little wordlings

he calmed his
busy brain.

Since when the sun
is shining,

why worry it will rain?

So he shared his little picnic
with the lizard in the sun,
And they laughed at all their worrying and
REALLY had some fun.

Since when you're in the moment, there's
no need to run or hide.

And **THEN**
the only
butterflies...

... will be the ones outside.